D0523322

To Pop, with love.

K.W.

Published by Hodder Children's Books 1996

10 9 8 7 6 5 4 3 2 1

ISBN 0 340 65135 0 (PB)
0 340 63436 7 (HB)

Printed in Singapore

Hodder Children's Books
A division of Hodder Headline plc
338 Euston Road
London NW1 3BH

Imagine you are a
CROCODILE

Karen Wallace
Mike Bostock

A division of Hodder Headline plc

Imagine you are a crocodile.
A huge, hungry crocodile lies in a swamp.
The swamp is soupy and green.
Flies buzz in the sunshine.

The crocodile hangs in the water like a rotten log. Her two yellow eyes seem to float on the scum.

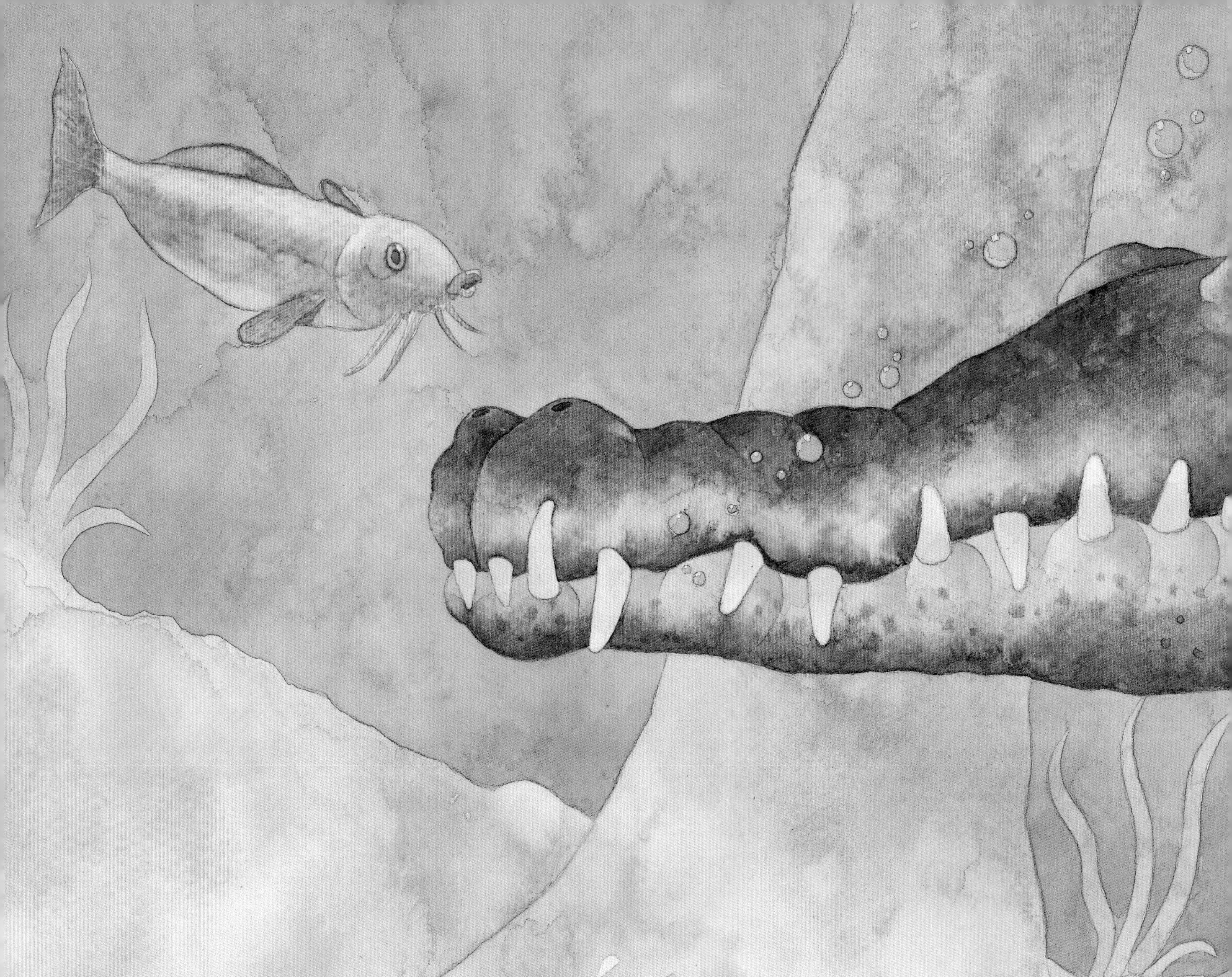

A huge, hungry crocodile sinks underwater.
She waits for a catfish to swim from the shallows.
The crocodile is lazy. She is never in a hurry.
She lies in the water watching and waiting.

Imagine you are a crocodile,
a jaw-snapping crocodile.
Suddenly a heron flies over the swamp.
The crocodile jumps.
She seems to stand on the water,
and snatches the heron
as it flies past her snout.

Imagine you are a crocodile, a full-bellied crocodile.
She turns in the water and glides to the bank.
Other crocodiles are resting. She climbs in among them.

The crocodile yawns.
Her mouth is huge as a cave.
Small birds peck for food
between her sharp teeth.
She closes her eyes
and sleeps in the sun.

On the edge of the swamp,
a snake drops from a branch.
It slides through the rushes
to a mound of dried grass.
Hidden inside are the crocodile's eggs.
She laid them in the summer.
Now they are ready to hatch.

Imagine you are a crocodile asleep in the sunshine.

The sound of tiny barks floats down from the rushes.

Inside their eggs, her babies are calling.

The snake slithers closer.

The crocodile wakes.

She ploughs through the reeds,
clambers on to her nest.
Then she digs out the eggs
with her short stubby claws.
Imagine you are a crocodile,
a fierce mother crocodile.
Her babies saw through their shells
and squeeze themselves out.

She carries them in her mouth
down to the water. Her babies are tiny
but their teeth are like needles.
They learn to catch flies
and crack open beetles.

Imagine you are a crocodile, a watchful mother crocodile.
In the night when the swamp is steamy and black,
Other crocodiles hunt like wolves in the water.
In the darkness an owl hoots.
A lizard rustles in the grass.
Mother crocodile keeps her babies safely beside her.

A long, scaly crocodile lies on a mudbank.
Her skin is her armour.
Her teeth are her weapons.
She looks like a dragon asleep in the sun.

Imagine you are a crocodile.